P9-DDD-867

For Blair Drawson,
my mutual cog in the wheel of fate

DK

DK Publishing, Inc., 375 Hudson Street, New York, New York 10014
Visit us on the World Wide Web at http://www.dk.com
Text and illustrations copyright © 2000 by Denys Cazet

Library of Congress Cataloging-in-Publication Data
Cazet, Denys.
Minnie and Moo and the Thanksgiving Tree / by Denys Cazet. — 1st ed.
p. cm.
"A DK Ink book."
Summary: All the animals in the barnyard ask the cows Minnie and Moo to hide
them so that they will not become Thanksgiving dinner.
ISBN 0-7894-2654-4 (hc)   ISBN 0-7894-2655-2 (pb)
[1. Cows—Fiction.   2. Domestic animals—Fiction.   3. Thanksgiving Day—Fiction.]   I. Title
PZ7.C2985Mf   2000   [E]—dc21   00-021278

The illustrations for this book were created with pencil and watercolor.
The illustration on these pages was drawn in pencil.
The text of this book is set in 18 point Berling.
Printed and bound in China by L.Rex Printing Co., Ltd.
First edition, 2000
6 8 10 9 7 5

Minnie and Moo

and the
Thanksgiving Tree

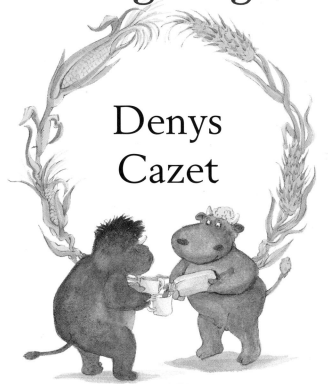

Denys
Cazet

DK PUBLISHING, INC.

Zeke and Zack

Minnie and Moo sipped hot cocoa.

The autumn sky was cold and clear.

Minnie ate a cream puff.

"You were saying?" she said.

Moo looked out over the farm.

"We have so much to be thankful for—

and yet I feel a sadness in the air."

Suddenly two turkey heads
popped out of the tall grass.

"You can say that again!"
said the first turkey.
"You can say that again!"
said the second turkey.
They ducked down.

"What was that?" said Minnie.

"The Beakerson brothers," said Moo.

"Zeke?" Moo called. "Zack?"

The turkeys peeked out of the grass.

"Ssshhh!" said Zeke.

They looked back at the farmer's house.

"Keep it down!" said Zack.

"What is their problem?"

Minnie muttered.

"It's Thanksgiving morning,"

said Moo.

Minnie rolled her eyes.

"Here we go again!"

Thanksgiving Jitters

Zeke and Zack crept out of the grass.

"Hide us," said Zeke.

"On the moon," said Zack.

"What?"

"We heard you went there," said Zeke.

"On a tractor," said Zack.

"Thanksgiving jitters," said Minnie.

"Relax!" said Moo. "The farmer's wife hasn't cooked a Thanksgiving turkey in years."

"Relax?" said Zeke.

"Can't," said Zack.

"Company coming," said Zeke.

"Pluckers and Stuffers," said Zack.

"What?"

"Mrs. Farmer's cousins from the city are here for a Thanksgiving visit," said Moo.

"Hide us," said Zeke.

"On the moon," said Zack.

"I have an idea," said Moo.

She whispered in Minnie's ear.

Minnie nodded.

"We will help you," she said.

"We will hide you high in the sky.

You will see the moon."

"Thank you," said Zeke.

"Thank you," said Zack.

The turkeys ran to the edge of the grass.

"They will hide us in the sky,"

whispered Zeke.

"We will see the moon,"

whispered Zack.

Thirty-six turkeys

popped out of the grass.

"Thank you!" they all whispered.

The Chickens

Minnie and Moo watched
the last turkey climb
into the old oak tree.
They looked at all the turkeys
sitting above them in the branches.
"I think we should move," said Moo.
"Good idea," said Minnie.

They sat down at the edge of the grass.

"Now, you were saying?" said Minnie,

eating another cream puff.

"I was saying, there is a sadness—"

"Hey, cows," whispered the rooster,

stepping out of the tall grass.

A flock of chickens

gathered behind him.

"Listen, cows! The turkeys are gone!"

"So?" said Minnie.

"Geez," said the rooster.

"And they say chickens are dumb!

The food chain . . . get it?

No turkey . . . chicken is next."

Minnie did not like the rooster.

"You cows have to hide us,"

said the rooster.

"After all, I make the sun come up!"

Minnie glared at him.

"Up there!" she said,

pointing at the tree.

"Come on, girls!" said the rooster.

They flew into the tree.

"Hey!" he shouted.

"I found the turkeys."

Minnie jumped up.

"Oh!" she yelled.

"Moo, is that the farmer I see?"

The tree was quiet.

Moo looked around.

She did not see the farmer.

"Minnie . . ."

Minnie sat down. "You were saying?"

"Ohhh," said Moo.

"Well . . . I was saying—"

"Pssst!" said a voice.

The Big Bird

An ostrich peeked out of the grass.

"Did you hear?" she asked.

"The turkeys

AND the chickens are missing!"

"WE HEARD!" said a duck,

six geese, two pigs,

and a flock of sheep hiding in the grass.

19

"You know what that means!"
said the duck.
"It means someone is going to want
to nibble on a hunk of ham,"
said a pig, slapping his bottom.
Moo tried to explain.
"The farmer's wife hasn't—"
"Where can we hide?" said a goose.
"Please," said Moo. "Listen—"
"There!" said the duck. "In that tree."
"What a good idea," said the ostrich.
They ran to the tree and climbed up.

"Hey!" shouted the ostrich.

"I found the turkeys . . .

and there are the chickens!"

"Ssshhh," said Zeke.

"Keep it down," said Zack.

"Cool it!" said the rooster.

Moo jumped up.

"Is that the farmer I see?"

The tree was quiet.

Minnie looked at the farmhouse.

She did not see the farmer.

She winked at Moo.

"So," she said,

taking another cream puff

out of the box.

"You were saying, Moo?"

"I was saying—"

"Pssst," said a voice.

Bea and Madge

The Holsteins peeked out of the grass.

"Bea!" said Moo.

"Madge! What are you doing?"

"Hiding," said Bea.

"Didn't you hear?" Madge said.

"Turkeys, pigs, chickens,

geese, sheep, ducks . . . gone!"

"And an ostrich," added Minnie.

"In the oak tree," said Moo.

Bea and Madge looked up.

"What a great idea," said Madge.

"Help us with our luggage!"

"That is a steamer trunk," said Moo.

"A *big* steamer trunk," said Minnie.

"Our overnight things are in here,"
said Bea.

"Bea, Madge, listen to us—"

"Please," said Madge.

"Help us climb into the tree."

Moo sighed.

Minnie shrugged.

She helped Moo climb into the tree.

"I will pull," said Moo.

"Minnie will push."

Moo pulled and pulled.

Minnie pushed and pushed.

Soon Bea, Madge,

and the steamer trunk were in the tree.

"Help me down," said Moo.

"Wait!" said Bea. "I found the turkeys—

AND the chickens AND—"

"Put a sock in it!" said the rooster.

"MOO!" Minnie yelled. "LOOK!

HERE COMES THE FARMER!"

Moo looked.

She saw Mr. and Mrs. Farmer

and the city cousins walking up the hill.

"Quick!" said Moo. "Help me down!"

"Too late!" Minnie cried.

"Help me up!"

"Madge, Bea, hurry!" said Moo.

"PULL! PULL! PULL!"

Minnie flopped over the lowest branch.

"There!" she huffed.

"Now the other end!"

They pulled and pulled.

"I thought you were on a diet,"

grunted Madge.

"I am," Minnie wheezed.

"The cream-puff diet.

Moo read about it in a magazine."

"PULL!" said Moo. "PULL!"

The Picnic

Mrs. Farmer stood

under the old oak tree.

"Here," she said.

"This is the perfect place

for our Thanksgiving picnic.

John, you spread out the blanket.

Emma and Lulu, you put out the food."

Mrs. Farmer lifted a lid.

"Surprise!" she said.

"I made a tofu loaf

in the shape of a turkey."

The farmer stared at the platter.

"Tofu?" Emma said. "What is tofu?"

"Mashed bean crud," said the farmer.

"*Curd*," said the farmer's wife.

"Not crud!"

"Yum!" whispered Zeke.

"Yum!" whispered Zack.

"Pipe down!" hissed the rooster.

Lulu looked up at the tree.

"Did you hear that?"

"I heard the tree speak!" said Emma.

"What?" said the farmer, tapping his
hearing aid.

Lulu raised her arms to the tree.

"Speak to us, O great and noble oak!"

Emma raised her arms.

"Send us a message, O wise one!"

An ostrich egg tumbled out of the tree.

It plopped into the tofu loaf.

"Ohhh!" gasped Emma and Lulu.

They ran to the tree and hugged it.

"This is a Thanksgiving tree,"

said Lulu.

The Thanksgiving Tree

Emma looked into the tree.

"This tree is magic," she said.

"I wonder what else it grows?"

She jerked on a curly branch.

A pig popped out.

"I picked a pig," said Emma proudly.

Lulu picked up her cup.

"I think I'll have something to drink."

She pushed her cup into the branches.

"Oh!" whispered Madge.

"What's the matter?"

whispered Minnie.

"Something just pulled on my udder!"

"Oh!" whispered Bea. "Mine, too!"

Lulu looked into her cup.

"This tree gives milk," she said.

"This is a Thanksgiving tree,"
said Emma.

"This is the tree of milk and honey!"

"You need *cows* to give milk!"
said the farmer.

"And *bees* to make honey!"

"Bees?" whispered the rooster.

"Did you hear that? BEES!"

"BEES!" shouted the turkeys.

"THIS TREE IS FULL OF BEES!"

Suddenly the tree exploded.

Animals fell.

They flew.

They jumped.

They squawked.

They quacked.

They squealed.

The steamer trunk
bounced out of the tree.

Then . . . all was quiet.

"Well," said Mrs. Farmer.

"I think *this* picnic is over.

Let's go back to the house.

I made cream puffs for dessert."

Happy Thanksgiving

Minnie and Moo

sat high in the old oak tree.

"I knew it," said Moo.

"There are no bees!"

Minnie held tightly to the tree.

"Bees or no bees," she said,

"I'm not moving!"

Minnie and Moo

looked out over the farm.

They watched the rising harvest moon.

"So," said Minnie.

"You were saying?"

"We have so much to be thankful for—

and yet I feel a sadness in the air."

Minnie looked down.

The ground seemed very far away.

She sat closer to Moo.

"Summer has summered,

fall has fallen,

and cold winter is coming," said Moo.

"Things come and things go."

"Like cream puffs," said Minnie sadly.

"Yes," said Moo. "Like cream puffs.

There is the joy of having

and the sadness of not having . . .

like summer and winter."

Minnie sighed.

"Spring brings hope," said Moo.

"And maybe more cream puffs,"

said Minnie.

Moo put her arm around Minnie.

"Exactly," she said. "Even winter

is made warmer by friendship."

Minnie smiled.

"Happy Thanksgiving," she said.

"Happy Thanksgiving," said Moo.